LauRa D.
and heR Veggies

A story about little Laura D
and how her veggies make
her bum sing.

Hi!
My name is Laura D. and I LOVE my veggies.
I know what you're thinking...

How could I possibly enjoy eating
such scary looking food?

These strange shapes and colours
that we're too afraid to chew?

Well one day my Mother asked me,
"Are you a brave girl?"
"I'm the bravest girl in the world,"
I said with a twirl.

"Then you'll try a different
vegetable for one week, each night.
Monday to Sunday and promise to
not put up a fight."

I shook my mom's hand...
And the journey began....

It all started with...

BROCCOLI
MONDAY

Kids aren't supposed to eat little green trees!
But when I was brave enough to try it...

My bum buzzed like a bumble bee!

BZZZzzT!

CAULIFLOWER TUESDAY

Who would ever want to eat little white brains!
But when I was brave enough to try it...

My bum honked like a choo-choo train!

BRUSSEL SPROUT
WEDNESDAY

Kids aren't supposed to eat little green eyeballs!
But when I was brave enough to try it...

My bum was so loud that it shook the walls!

SWEET POTATO
THURSDAY

Who would ever want to eat orange and brown lumps!
But when I was brave enough to try it...

I was so stinky, my dog thought I ate a skunk!

CORN FRIDAY

Kids aren't supposed to... wait a minute.
Corn doesn't make you toot.

But it sure does show up the next day in your poop!

ASPARAGUS
SATURDAY

Who would ever want to eat a Giant's long green fingers!
But when I was brave enough to try it...

I tooted just once actually... But boy did it linger!

GREEN PEA
SUNDAY

Kids aren't supposed to eat green bunny poo!
But when I was brave enough to try it...

My bum woke up my poor Grandma too!

Can you guess why I had such an amazing week?
That's right! These veggies made my bum squeak.

Vegetables are great and will make you strong.
So deep in your belly is where they belong.
As you put more of them into your tummy...
You'll realize that they are quite yummy.

You must say excuse me, that is all that I ask.
Now go tell your family to get some gas masks.
Bye! Or should I say...

Tootaloo!